A Sister More Like Me

by Barbara Jean Hicks

illustrated by Brittney Lee

Disney PRESS
New York • Los Angeles

To Laurel and Lindy, the two best sisters in the world
—B.J.H.

To Lainey, my little sister and source of endless inspiration
—B.L.

Copyright © 2013 Disney Enterprises, Inc. All rights reserved. Published by
Disney Press, an imprint of Disney Book Group. No part of this book may be
reproduced or transmitted in any form or by any means, electronic or mechanical,
including photocopying, recording, or by any information storage and retrieval
system, without written permission from the publisher. For information address
Disney Press, 1101 Flower Street, Glendale, California 91201.
Printed in the United States of America
First Edition
10 9 8 7 6 5 4
F322-8368-0-14127
ISBN 978-1-4231-7014-3
Library of Congress Control Number: 2013931930
Designed by Winnie Ho

Visit www.disneybooks.com

My name is
Princess Elsa.
I'm as royal as can be.

If the words look neat
and purple, then they
belong to me.

I'm her little sister,
Anna—I like color,
noise, and shine.

When the words are pink
and crowded, you can tell
that they are mine.

When you and I were little,
we were close as we could be.

I was happy you were Anna.
You were thrilled that I was me.

Till I had to hide my magic,
and our closeness
had to end.

I was still your older sister,
but I couldn't be your friend.

I followed you
around the house

and chattered like a bird.

I tried my best to please you,
but you never said a word.

That's when I started dreaming about
how my life would be . . .
if I ever had a chance to have
a sister more like me.

I considered it my job to do what
needed to be done.
You were always and forever finding
ways to have more fun.

There were times you made me crazy,
though I tried to let you be—
as I wondered why I couldn't have
a sister more like me.

While I galloped on my pony
in the wind and rain and sun,
you were cooped up in the study—
and you thought that it was fun!

I'd have loved to have a playmate
who would join me up a tree.
I would have, if I could have had
a sister more like me.

And *I'd* have loved to have a friend who knew geometry—
I would have, if I could have had a sister more like *me*.

You needed peace and quiet.

I was Princess Meet-and-Greet.

Your room was an explosion!

Mine was always clean and neat.

You were elegant and proper,
and you loved a fancy tea,

while I preferred a bright and breezy picnic by the sea.

You didn't seem to care a bit about the way you dressed.
It was important, as a princess, that I look my best.

You were the picture of perfection,
every day, no matter what.
I tried to understand you,
but the door was always shut.

Then one day I was so dazzled when I saw what you could be.
And I wondered . . . did I *really* want a sister more like me?

You showed me that you loved me,
and I suddenly felt free—
and truly glad I didn't have
a sister more like me.

You always did your duty,
and you always used your head.

You always listened to your heart
and followed where it led.

I'm very glad I *haven't* had a sister more like me.
With you around, without a doubt, I see things differently.

I was prickly as an urchin.
I was stubborn as a mule!
Now we try to work together—

it's our Sister Golden Rule.

You are bold and fearless, Sister,
and you have a loving heart.

You are poised and graceful, Sister,
and so wonderfully smart.

I'm so happy you are Anna, and I'm pleased that I am me.

I'm thrilled that you are Elsa, and I'm happy I am me!

But even more important—we are happy we are WE.